Book 5

CARNIVAL ON NEPTUNE

BY JEFF DINARDO
ILLUSTRATED BY DAVE CLEGG

RED
CHAIR
·PRESS·

Funny Bone Books

and Funny Bone Readers are produced and published by

Red Chair Press LLC   PO Box 333   South Egremont, MA 01258-0333

www.redchairpress.com

About the Author

Jeff Dinardo's books are filled with humor and silliness that captures a child's imagination. When not writing, Jeff runs a successful design firm specializing in textbooks for use in classrooms from K-8.

About the Artist

Dave Clegg lives and works on a small horse farm in north Georgia with his wife Lyn. All of Dave's work is done digitally on his computer. When he is not drawing, he can be found creating songs with his guitar or making robot sculptures!

Publisher's Cataloging-In-Publication Data

Names: Dinardo, Jeffrey. | Clegg, Dave, illustrator. | Dinardo, Jeffrey. Jupiter twins ; bk. 5.

Title: Carnival on Neptune / by Jeff Dinardo ; illustrated by Dave Clegg.

Other Titles: Funny bone books. First chapters.

Description: South Egremont, MA : Red Chair Press, [2019] | Interest age level: 005-007. | Summary: "Trudy and Tina make a great team and are excited about the Winter Carnival. But will there be enough snow and ice? Discover how the twins save the day for everyone."--Provided by publisher

Identifiers: ISBN 9781634407502 (library hardcover) | ISBN 9781634407540 (paperback) | ISBN 9781634407588 (ebook)

Subjects: LCSH: Twins--Juvenile fiction. | Neptune (Planet)--Juvenile fiction. | Outer space--Exploration--Juvenile fiction. | Carnival--Juvenile fiction. | CYAC: Twins--Fiction. | Pluto (Planet)--Fiction. | Outer space--Exploration--Fiction. | Carnival--Fiction.

Classification: LCC PZ7.D6115 Juc 2019 (print) | LCC PZ7.D6115 (ebook) | DDC [E]--dc23 | LCCN: 2018955670

Printed in United States of America

0519 1P CGF19

CONTENTS

Meet the Characters

Trudy

Tina

Ms. Bickleblorb

Ice Giants

🚀 1 No Snow

The Jupiter team's equipment was packed tightly into the space bus. It didn't leave a lot of room for the kids, but they didn't mind. They were excited about being asked to join this year's Winter Carnival.

Students from across the galaxy competed in competitions like ski racing, ice sculpting and even snowball making. Every year it was held on the icy slopes of Neptune.

Trudy and her twin sister Tina are co-captains of the team. Trudy is a natural skier and loves the feel of the cold wind blowing against her face as she races down the trails at home. Tina has been practicing her ice-carving skills.

"Remember to put on your hats and gloves," said Ms. Bickleblorb. "It's not just cold on Neptune. It's REALLY cold!"

Ms. Bickleblorb is not only their teacher, but their team coach too.

When they landed on Neptune, the twins and the rest of the team hopped off the space bus. But no cold air greeted them. It was warm.

"Hey, I thought it was supposed to be cold here," said Tina.

"How are we going to ski or make snowballs?" added Trudy.

The teams from the other planets had already arrived. They all looked sad.

An official-looking alien with a badge came over to Ms. Bickleblorb's team.

"I'm sorry," he said. "But without any snow, it looks like we have to cancel the Winter Carnival."

2 ICE GIANTS!

Before anyone could say a word, the air was filled with loud roars from behind the hills.

WAAAAA YAAAAAA YAAAA

All the kids jumped up to see what was going on. From behind a hill came three scary-looking creatures. Two were large and one was small. They looked like they were all made of ice. And they did not look happy.

"Ice Giants!" someone yelled. "We
heard they lived on Neptune, but no
one has ever seen them before."

The Ice Giants breathed freezing
cold air into their glistening ice claws.
The cold breath formed into snowballs,
which they threw down at the teams.

"Jumping Jupiter!" said Tina. "What
do we do now?"

"We RUN!" said Trudy as everyone
ran to hide.

All the teams were safely hidden as the
giant snowballs whizzed by in the air and
exploded into piles of snow on the ground.

After a few minutes the Ice Giants stopped their attack and slowly walked back out of sight. All the teams came out of hiding.

"It's time we all left!" said the alien with the official badge. "It seems we're not wanted here."

Trudy looked at the snowballs that littered the ground. She had an idea. She climbed onto a tall rock so she could be seen.

"Don't go yet," she shouted to all the teams. "I have an idea!"

"Oh no," sighed Tina. She knew her sister well.

3 CLIMBING

Before long Trudy and Tina were scaling the mountain in the direction that the Ice Giants had gone.

"What are we doing?" Tina said as she scaled another ridge.

"It's easy," said Trudy. "We need snow for the carnival to take place, right?"

"Right," sighed Tina.

"Well, those Ice Giants seem to be able to make snowballs any time they want," said Trudy. "All we need is to get them to make enough snow so we can still have the carnival!"

Tina looked shocked.

"But those Ice Giants were mad at us!" she said. "And we don't even know why!"

Trudy turned to start climbing the next ridge. "That is what we need to find out!" she said.

4 AT THE TOP

The twins finally reached the peak. They leaned against a boulder to catch their breath.

"I'm tired," puffed Tina. "That was some climb." All around them, the ground was filled with piles of white, fluffy snow.

"It's plenty cold here," said Tina.

"I think I know why," said Trudy as she pointed. There was a giant cave all made of ice. It glistened like diamonds.

"I think we found out where the Ice Giants live," said Trudy. "Come on."

The twins reached the opening of the cave and peeked inside. There didn't seem to be anyone home.

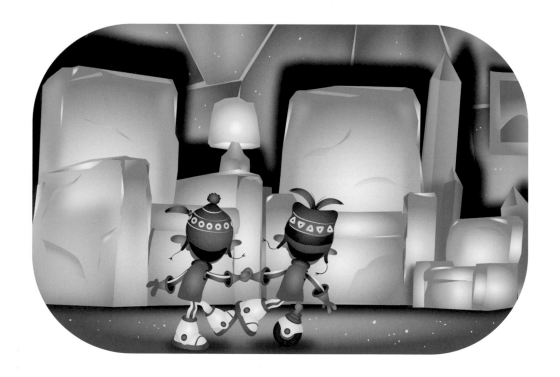

They decided to have a closer look. Inside they saw a large table with three chairs made of solid ice.

Trudy climbed up the big one and sat on it. "Too tall," she said.

Tina climbed on the middle chair and sat down. "Too cold," she said.

They both climbed up on the small chair and sat down together.

"Just right," they both said as they rested for a minute.

Then they ran up the icy steps and
saw a large room with three beds in it.
Trudy climbed into the first one.

"Too large," she said.

Tina climbed into the middle bed.

"Too hard," she said.

They both climbed into the small bed.
It had a nice fuzzy blanket on it.

"This is just right," they said as they
cuddled up together.

Soon they both fell asleep.

A RUDE AWAKENING

Trudy felt a cold claw nudge her. She pushed it aside.

Tina felt cold breath on her face. She pulled the blanket up more.

A loud voice filled the air. "WHAT ARE YOU DOING IN OUR HOUSE?"

Trudy and Tina woke right up.

It was the two large Ice Giants. And they did not look happy.

"Run!" shouted Tina.

She and Trudy sprinted out of the room, down the ice steps, and right out the front of the cave.

WHOA!

They both crashed into the small Ice Giant. She was no bigger than they were.

"Watch out," said the small Ice Giant. "You almost made me knock over my sculpture."

Trudy and Tina got up and saw what the small Ice Giant had made. It was beautiful.

"What is it?" asked Trudy.

"It's a Rock Muncher from Mars," said the little Ice Giant. "But I've never seen one in real life."

"Believe me," said Trudy. "That is just what they look like."

Trudy and Tina didn't notice the two big Ice Giants were now right behind them. One of them put an arm around the little one.

"Little Lucy is an amazing ice carver," said the mother Ice Giant. "But no one would ever know, since no one invites us to the winter carnival."

"Is that why you tried to scare everyone away?" asked Tina.

"It's not nice to be ignored," said the father Ice Giant.

Trudy had an idea.

"I think I know just what to do!"

The winter carnival was back on. The two parent Ice Giants took turns making it snow. The mother Ice Giant even won first place in the snowball-making contest.

Trudy came in third in the ski race.
Tina came in second in the ice
sculpture contest. But she didn't mind.

Little Lucy, the smallest Ice Giant,
came in first place.